LOOKING DOWN

LOOKING DOWN

BY STEVE JENKINS

HOUGHTON MIFFLIN COMPANY
BOSTON NEW YORK

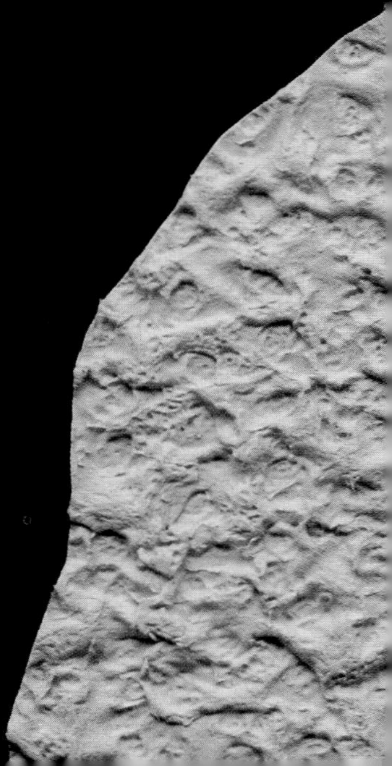

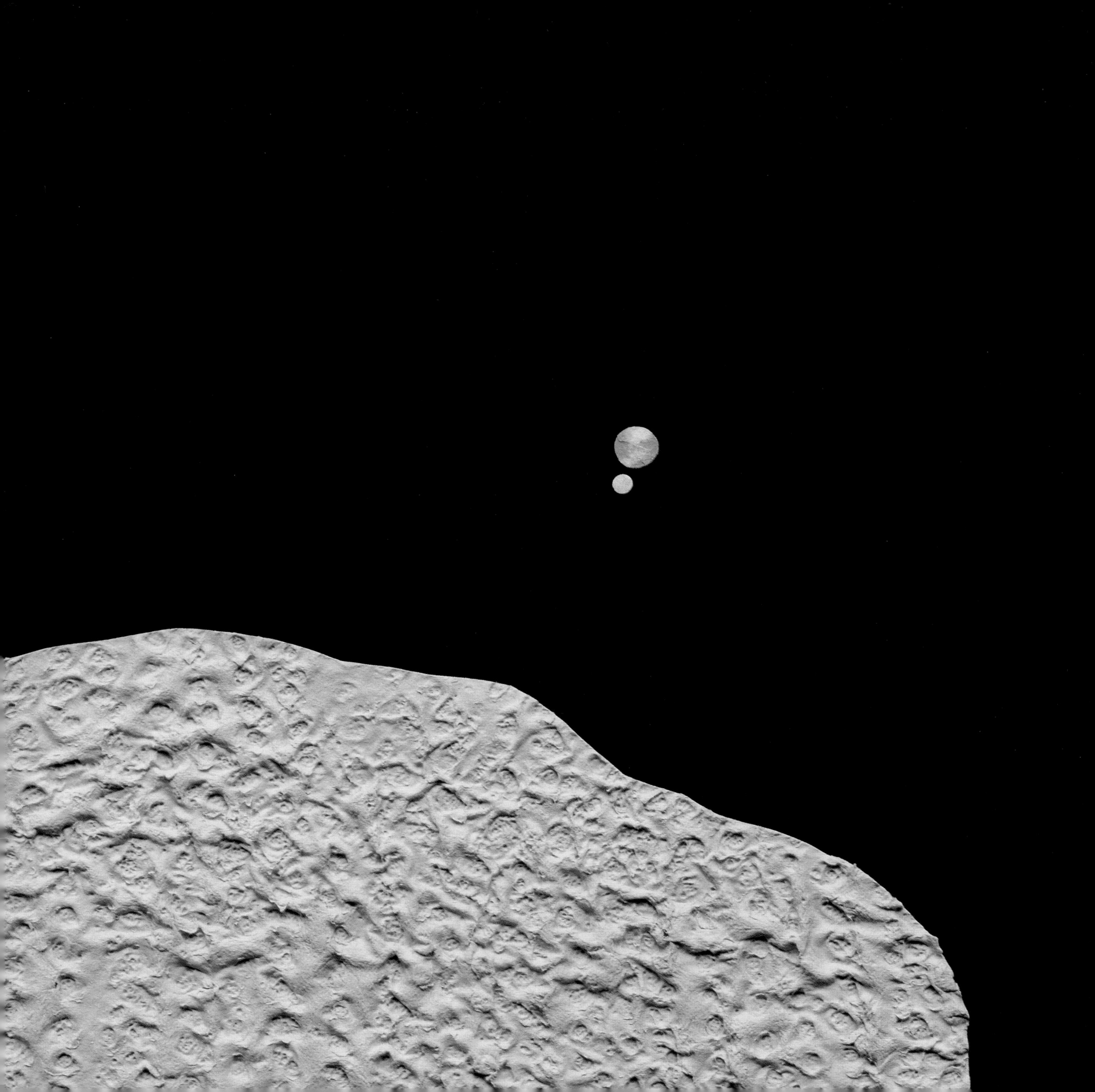

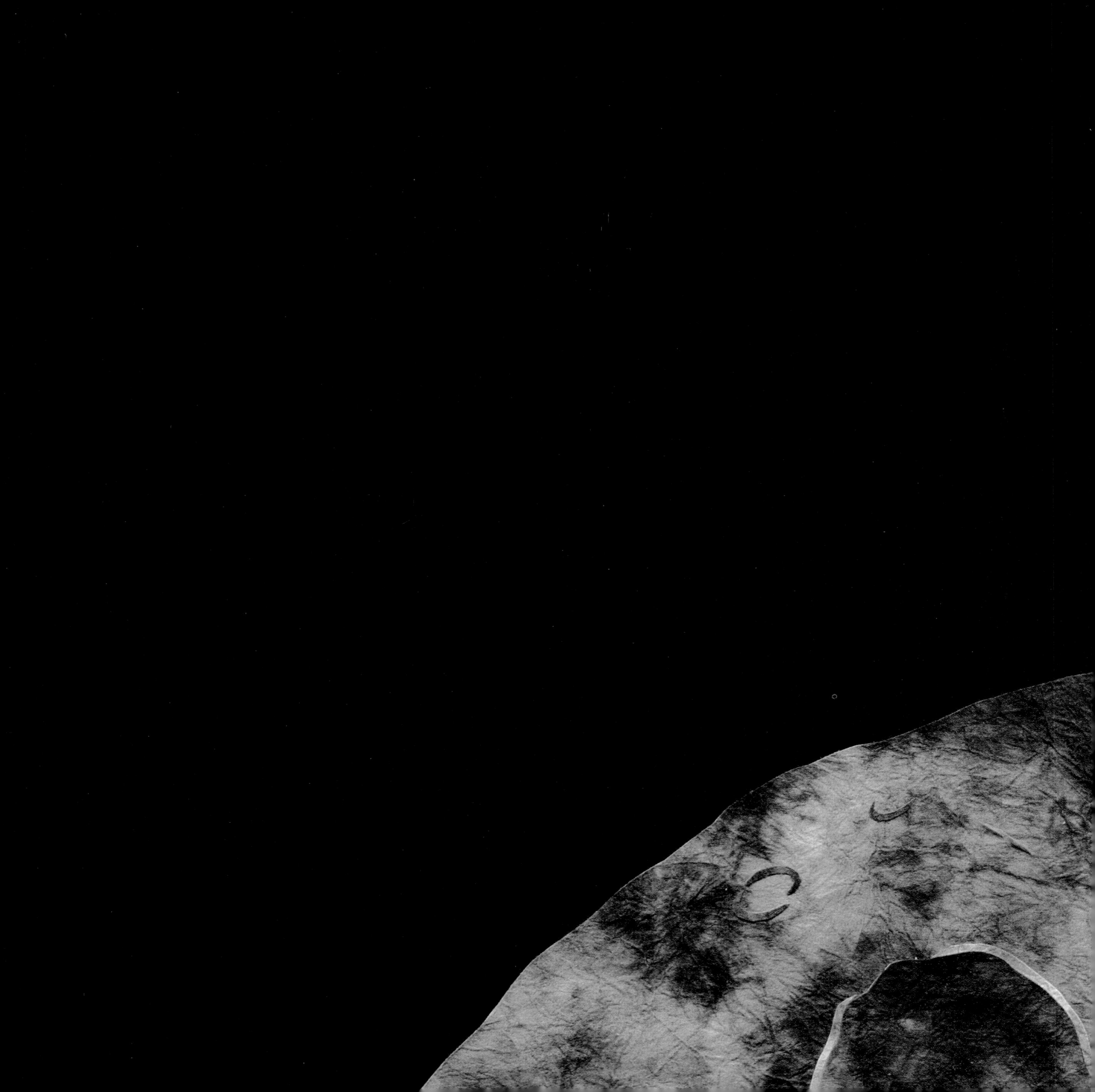

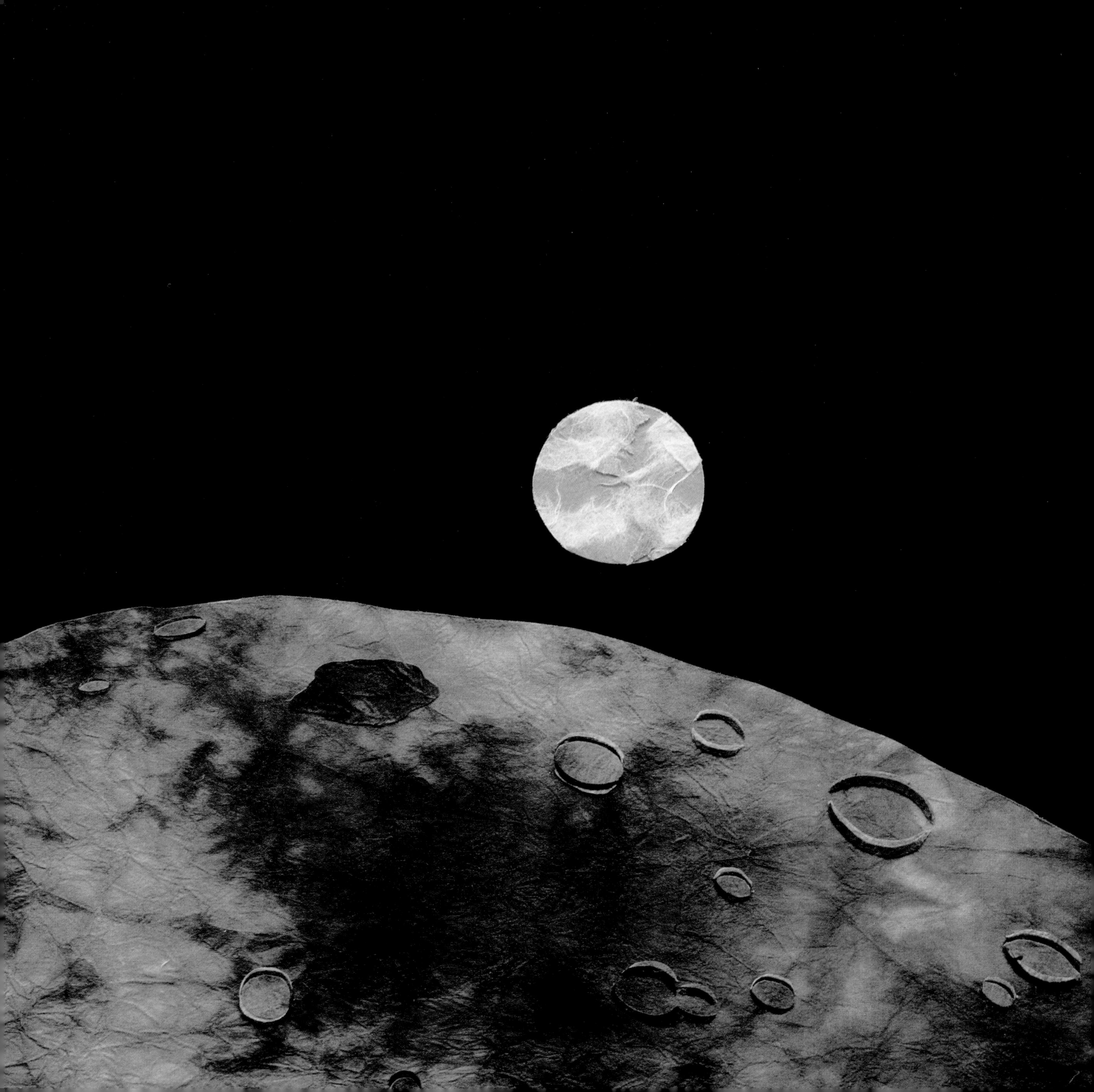

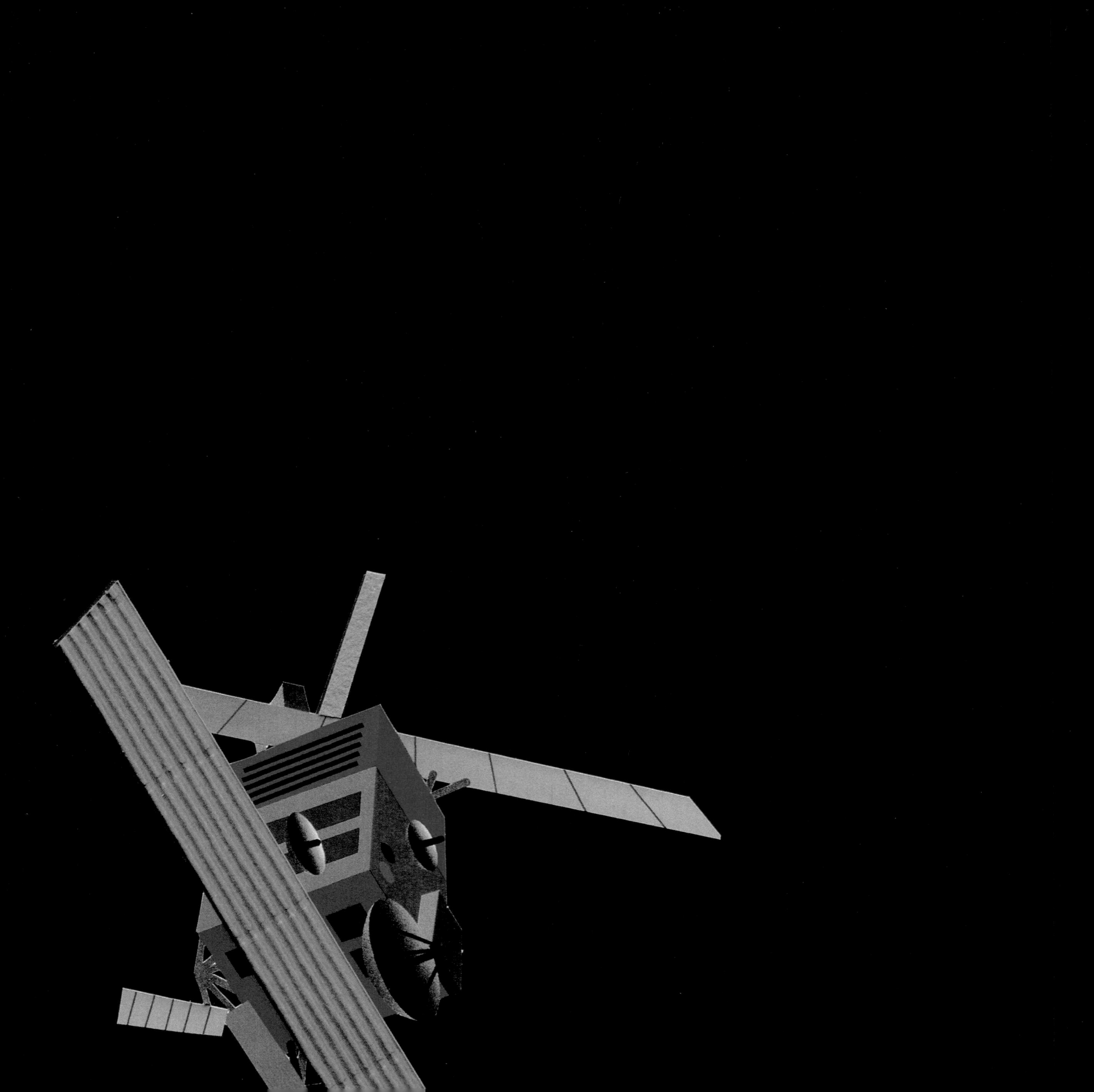

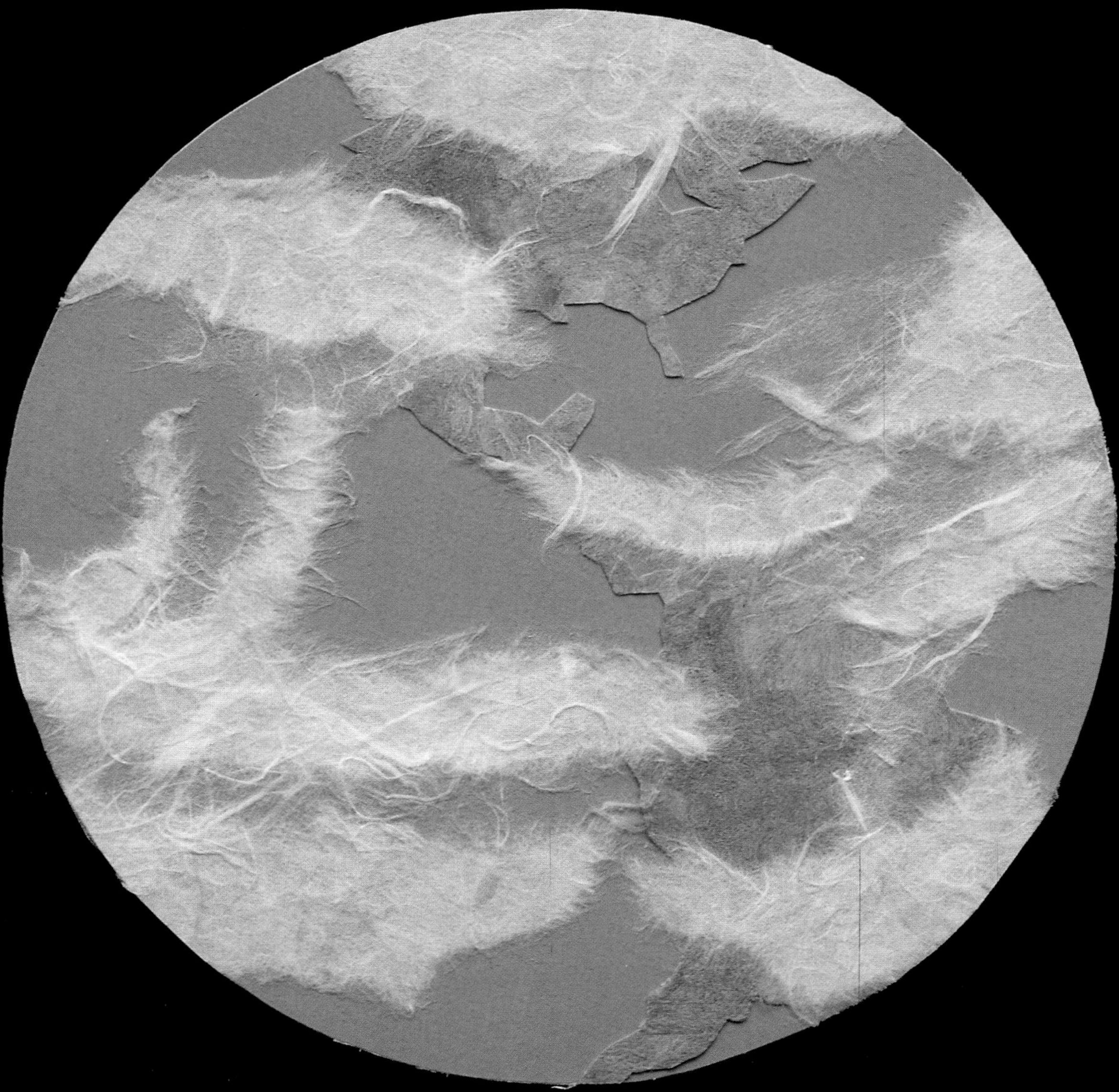

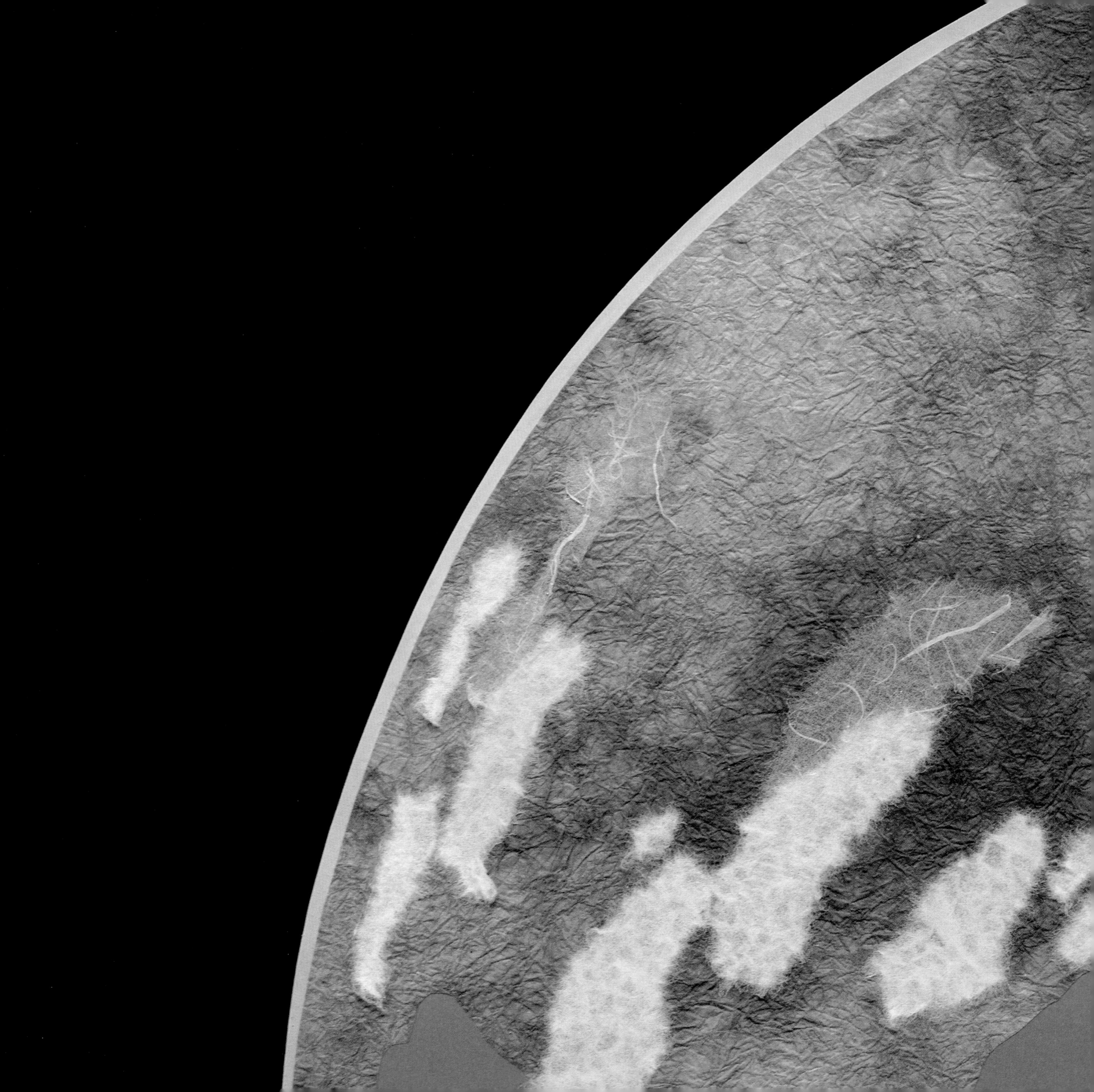

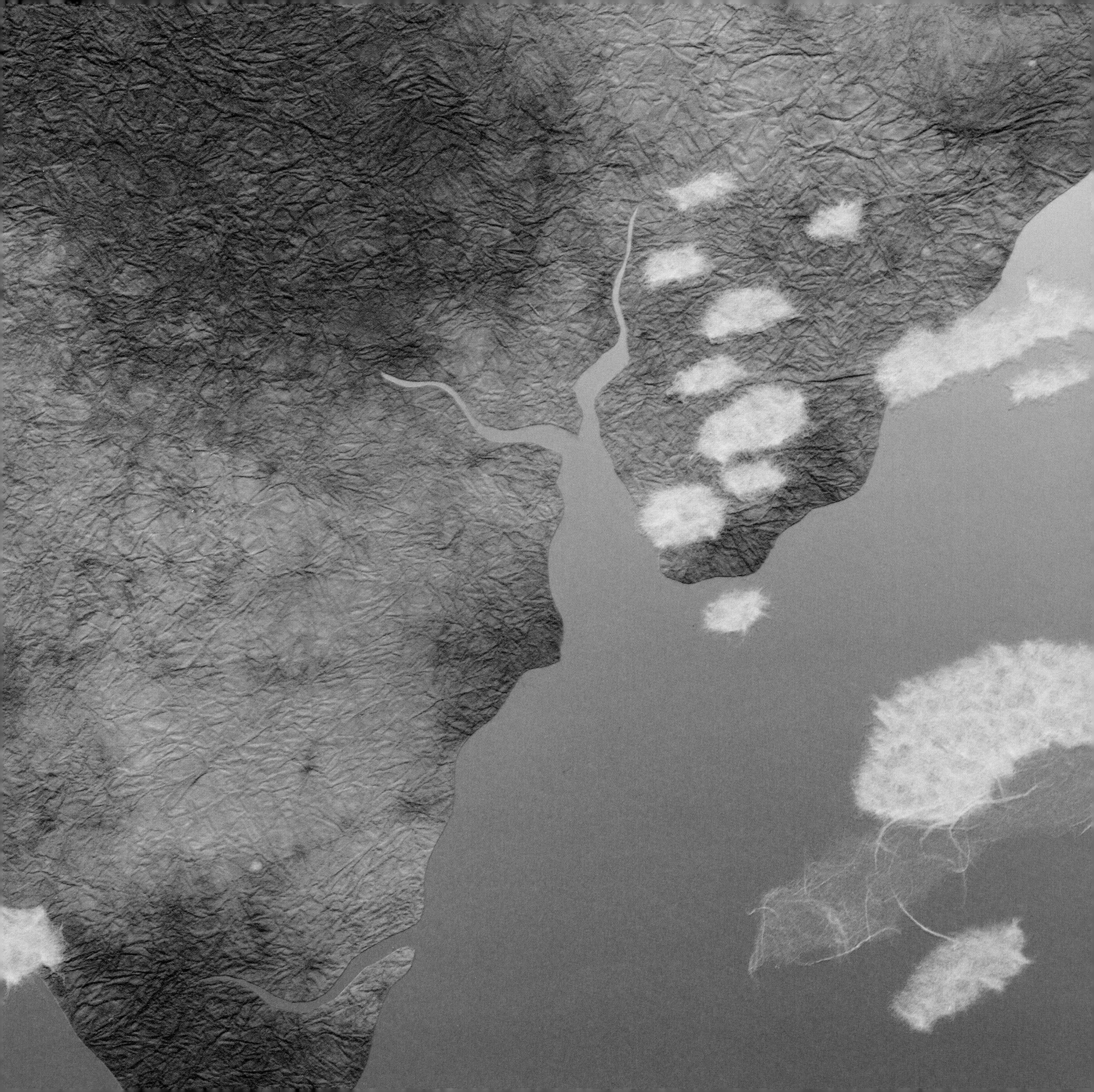

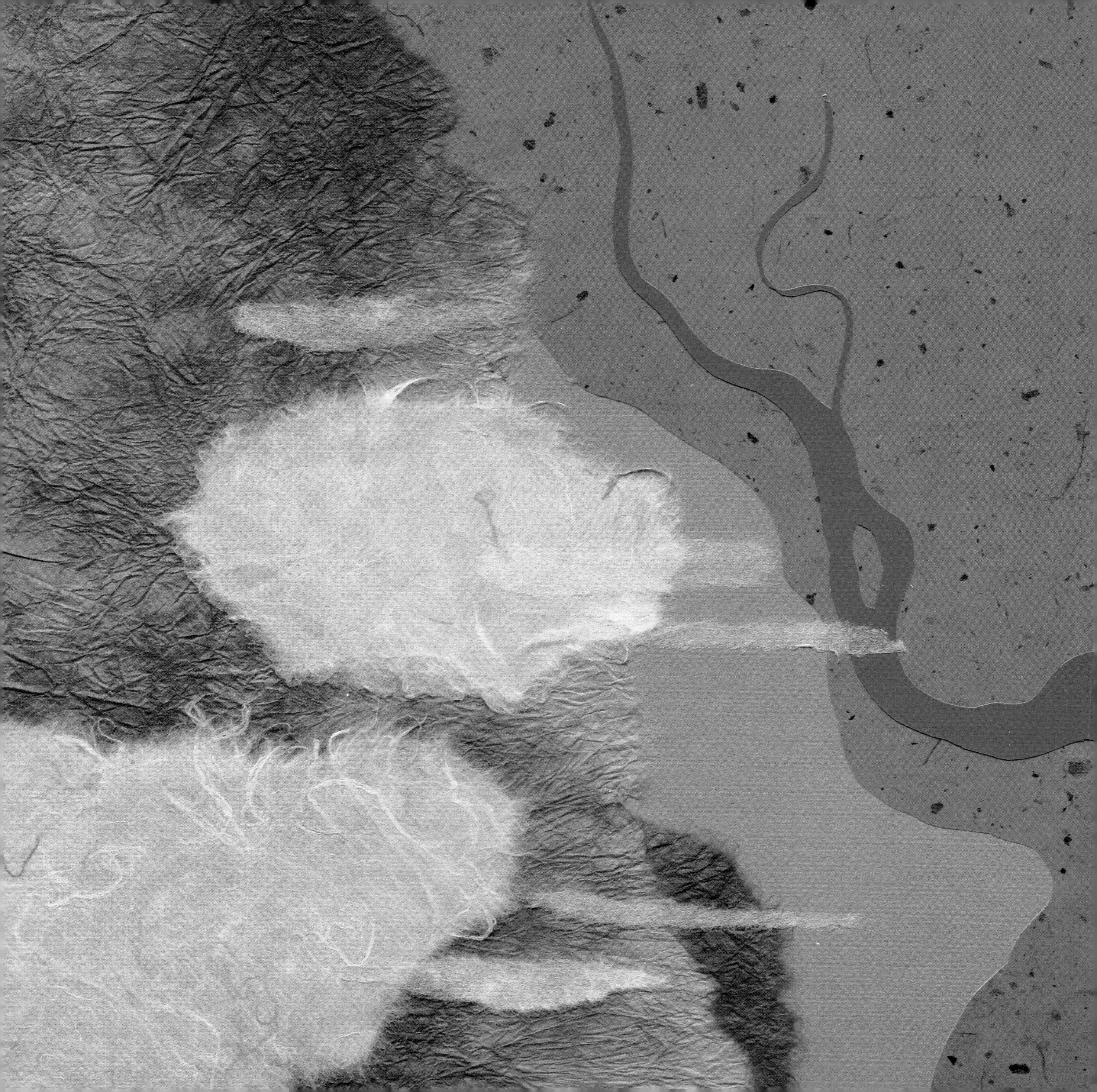

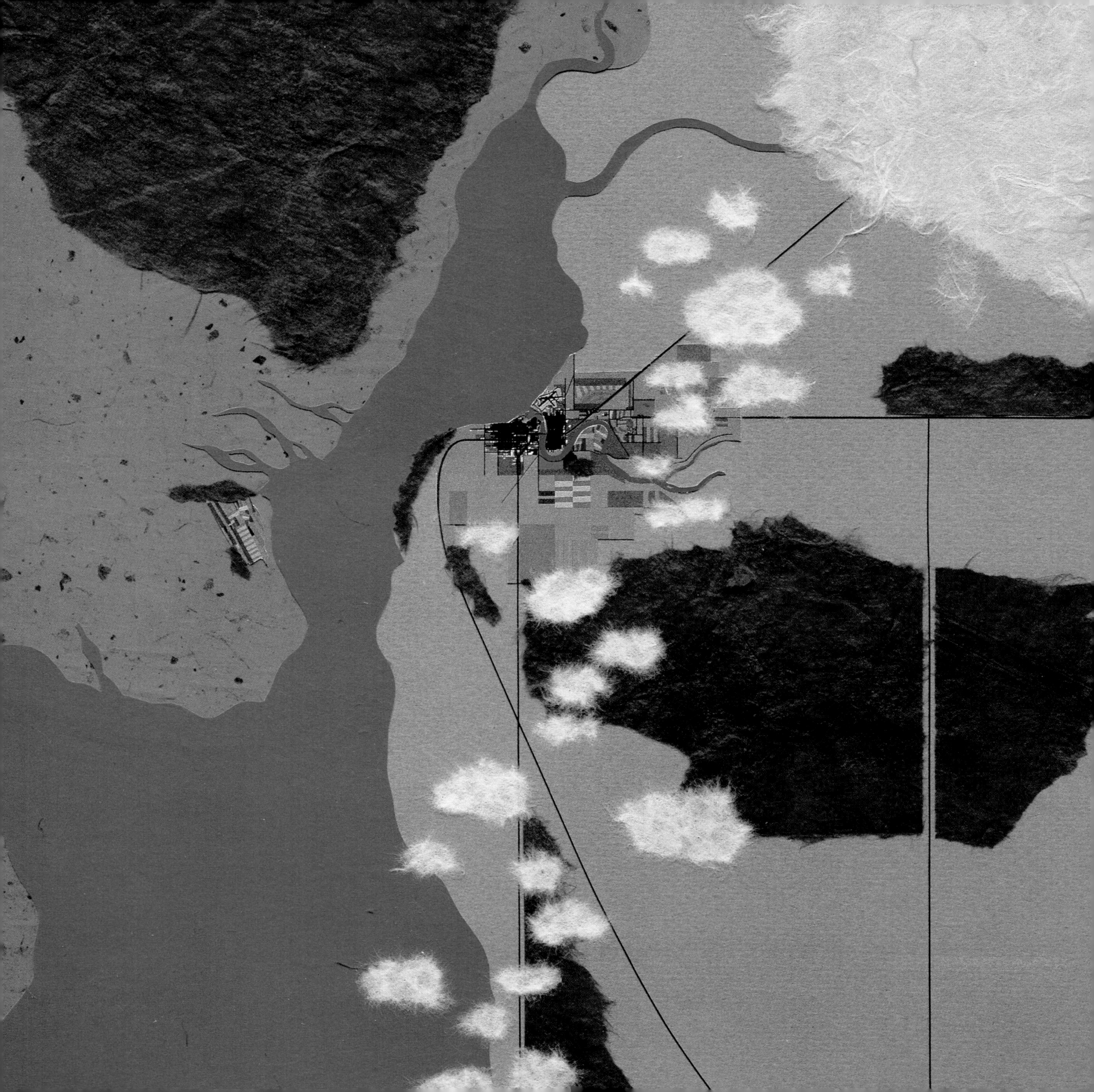

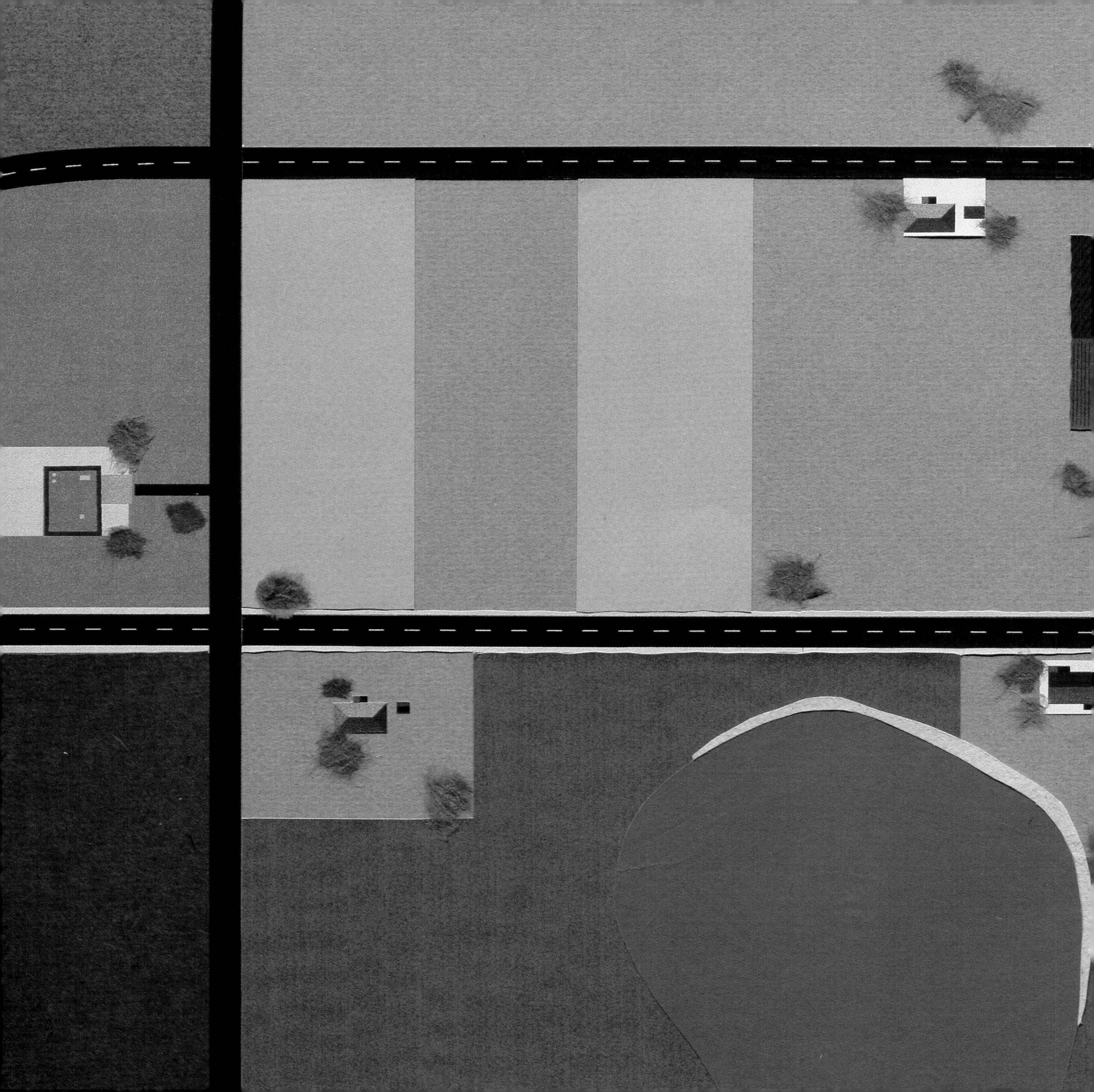

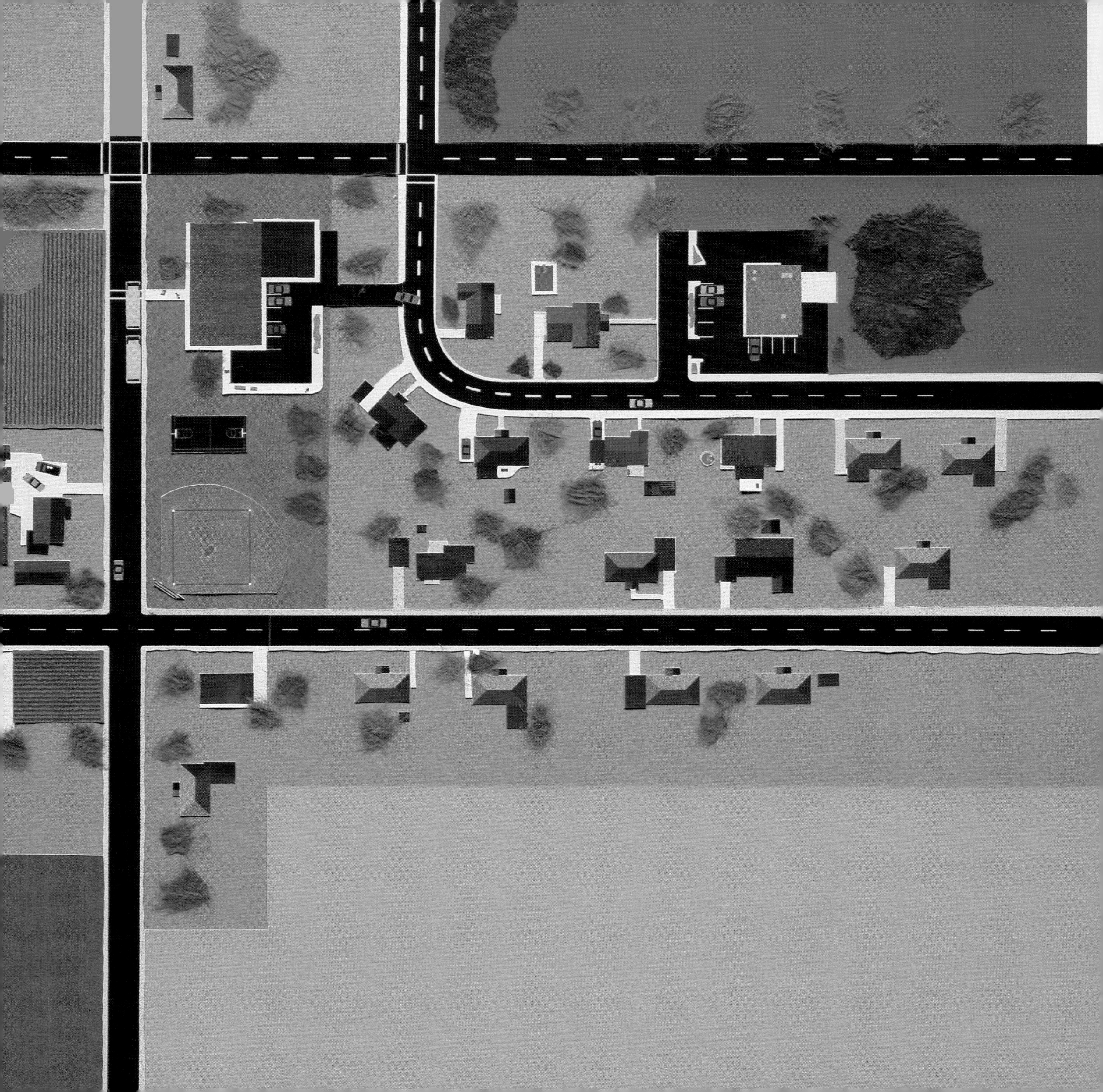

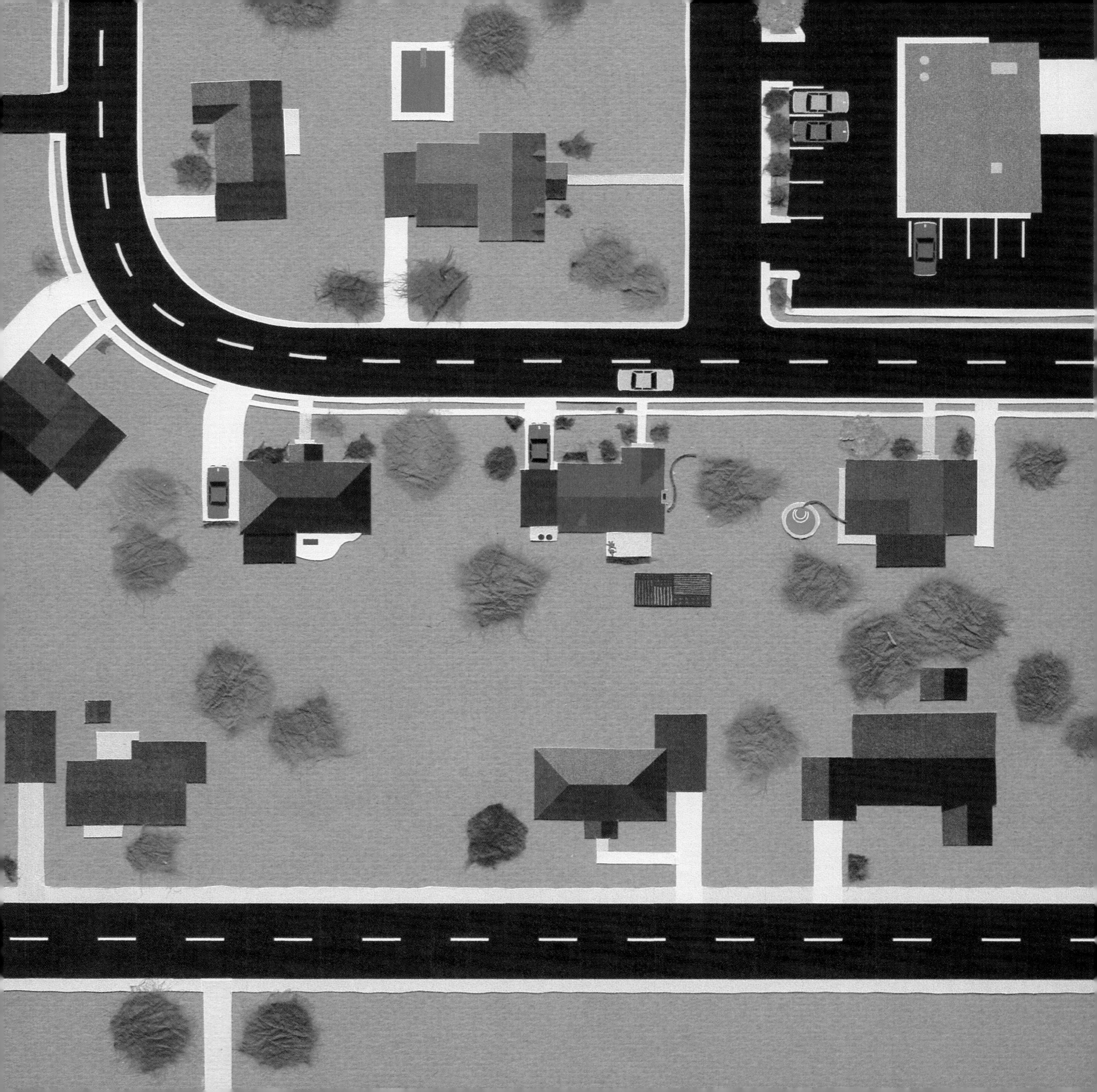

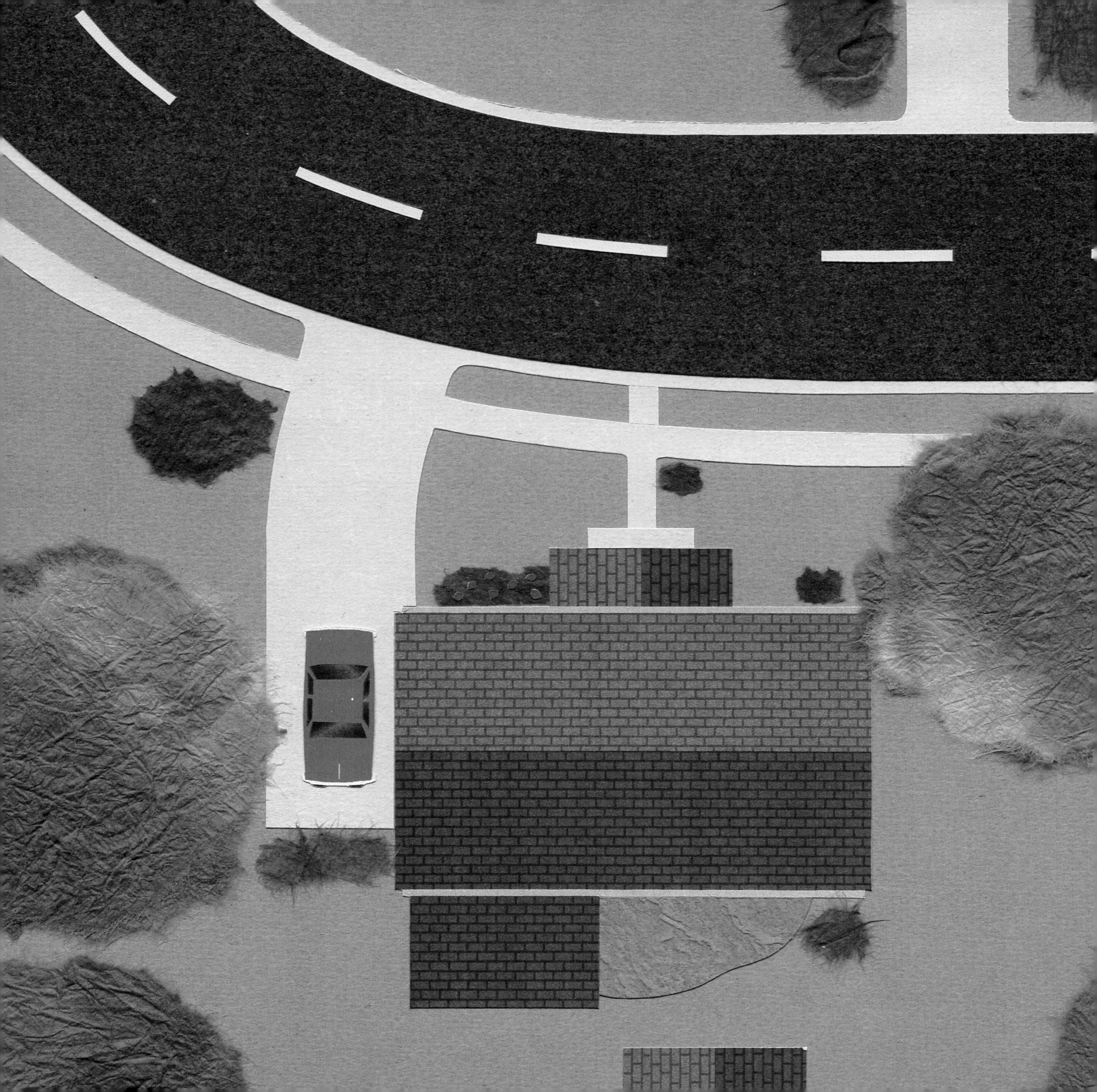

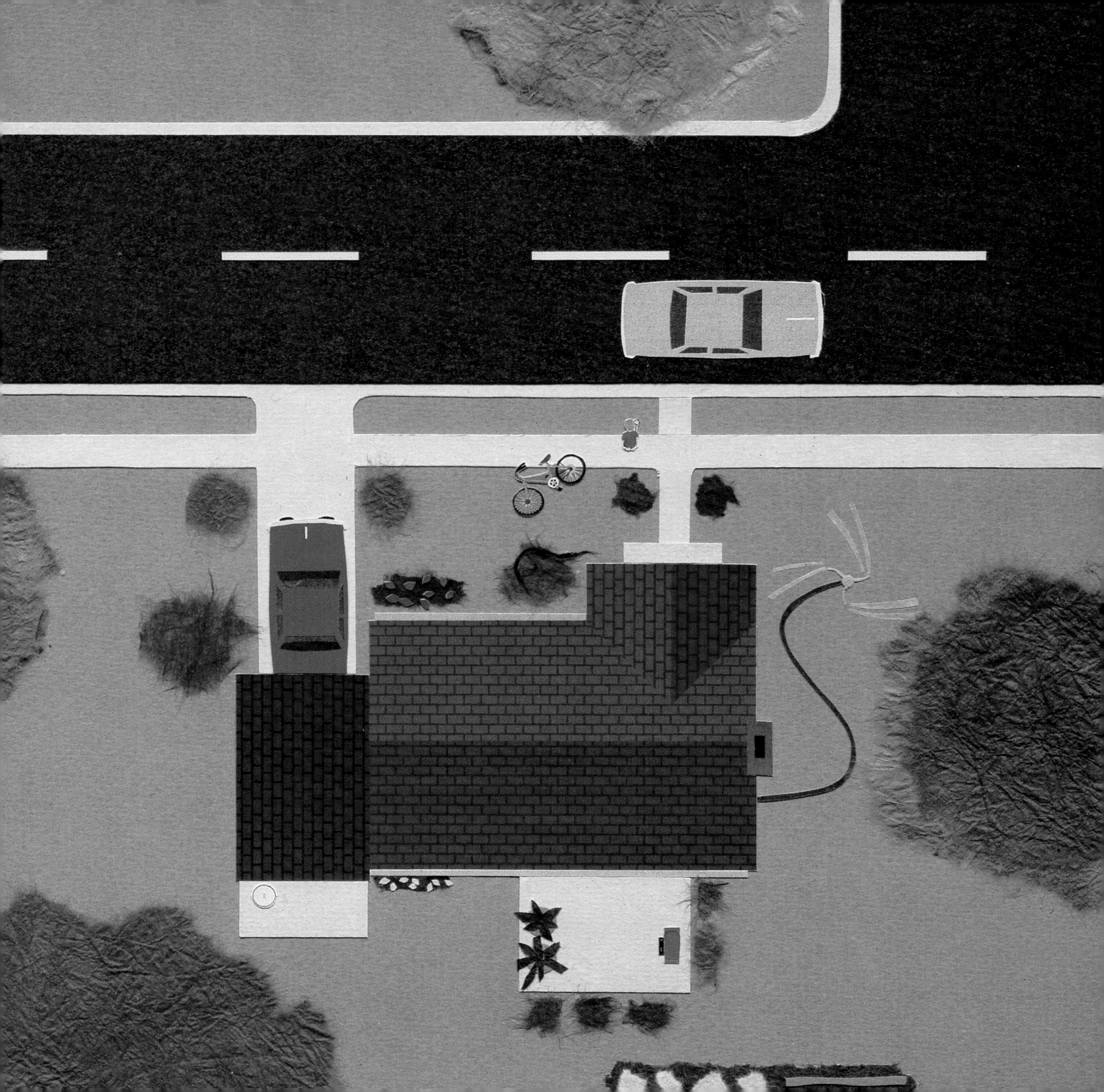

FOR MY MOTHER AND FATHER

The town we are "looking down" at in this book is not a real one, but it is like many towns on the East Coast of the United States between Maryland and South Carolina. In that part of the country, many farming communities have become big towns with more people and larger buildings.

 Manufactured in the United States of America. Book design by Steve Jenkins. The text of this book is set in Futura. The illustrations are cut-paper collages, reproduced in full color.
BVG 10 9 8 7 6 5 4 3 2

www.houghtonmifflinbooks.com

Library of Congress Cataloging-in-Publication Data Jenkins, Steve. Looking down / by Steve Jenkins. p. cm.
Summary: A series of views of one landscape is seen from progressively lower vantage points, beginning in outer space and ending with a view of a ladybug as seen by a kneeling child.
RNF ISBN 0-395-72665-4 PAP ISBN 0-618-31098-3
[1. Visual perception—Fiction.] I. Title. PZ7.J41737Lo 1995 [E]—dc20 94-38720 CIP AC